T0128030

The Ferengi
Rules of
Acquisition

By Quark
as told to
Ira Steven Behr

POCKET BOOKS

New York   London   Toronto   Sydney

An Original Publication of POCKET BOOKS

 POCKET BOOKS, a division of Simon and Schuster Inc.
1230 Avenue of the Americas, New York, NY 10020

Copyright © 1995 by Paramount Pictures. All Rights Reserved.

For information about special discounts for bulk purchases, please contact Simon & Schuster Special Sales: 1-800-456-6798 or business@simonandschuster.com

 STAR TREK is a Registered Trademark of Paramount Pictures.

A VIACOM COMPANY

This book is published by Pocket Books, a division of Simon & Schuster Inc., under exclusive license from Paramount Pictures.

ISBN: 978-0-671-52936-9

First Pocket Books trade paperback printing July 1995

10   9

POCKET and colophon are registered trademarks of Simon & Schuster Inc.

Cover design by Steve Ferlauto; cover photo by Tom Zimberoff

Printed in the U.S.A.

ACKNOWLEDGMENTS

Ira Steven Behr would like to thank the following people for their help with both the Rules of Acquisition and this book: Rick Berman, Michael Piller, Peter Allan Fields, James Crocker, Ronald D. Moore, Rene Echevarria, Evan Carlos Somers, David S. Cohen & Martin A. Winer, Sheri Lynn Behr, Michael & Denise Okuda, Robbin Slocum, Nell Crawford, Lolita Fatjo, Bob Gillan, John Ordover, Rick Schultz, and especially Robert Hewitt Wolfe, who knows these Rules as well as I do, and my wife, Laura Behr, who kept telling me "write the book, write the book."

Quark would like to thank Armin Shimerman, for reasons of a personal nature.

A FEW WORDS
FROM QUARK

Congratulations. I'm proud of you. You've made a wise purchase. The book you hold in your hands represents the sum total of Ferengi business wisdom. All right, maybe not the sum total. I suppose if you want to be technical what you're holding in your hands represents approximately one-quarter of the sum total of Ferengi business wisdom. If you're wondering how I reached that figure, it's really quite simple. You see, there are two hundred and eighty-five Rules of Acquisition. This book contains seventy—or about one-quarter of the total Rules. But believe me when I tell you, one-quarter of the sum total of Ferengi business wisdom is still a lot of wisdom. I doubt you humans could handle much more.

Now, I know what some of you are thinking. Just what *are* the Ferengi Rules of Acquisition? Good question. So for those of you who bought this book on the strength of the cover alone (and yes, that is your humble author standing there—have you ever seen such a devastating smile, such photogenic lobes?), I'd be happy to explain. The Rules of Acquisition consist of the two hundred and eighty-five guiding principles that form the basis of Ferengi business philosophy. A philosophy that has enabled the Ferengi people to become the most successful entrepreneurs in the galaxy. Think about it. Don't you want to increase your earning potential? Don't you want to make bigger, more lucrative business deals? Don't you want to double, triple, maybe even quadruple your profits?

I know I do.

And you do too.

Well then, this book is for you. Now, about these Rules . . .

Hold on!

YOU.

That's right, you! The one standing hunched over in that bookstore aisle reading this book. Stop! You heard me. I know what you're up to. You think you can read this entire book straight through, right there in that bookstore, then return it to the shelves and walk away having learned all its secrets WITHOUT COMPENSATING ITS AUTHOR. Well, I've got news for you, my friend: that's not how it works. Now, before you read another sentence I want you to close this book, carry it over to the salesperson ... AND PAY FOR IT. And while you're at it buy some copies for your friends. And your family. And any business colleagues you may have. Believe me, they need to own this book just as much as you do. So go ahead, buy a lot of copies. They'll thank you for it. And so will I.

Now don't let the slender size of this volume fool you. *The Ferengi Rules of Acquisition* is definitely *not* a book that can be read once and then tossed aside. Not if you truly want to profit from its lessons. No, the Rules are meant to be studied, weighed, evaluated, contemplated, mulled over, and reflected on until each word has been absorbed into your memory. In fact, I'd go so far as to say that *The Ferengi Rules of Acquisition* is the only book you need to own. Well, maybe not the only book. I'd also suggest you get yourself a copy of *The Ferengi Guide to Sexual Fulfillment: The Joys of Oo-moxing*. Anyone interested in purchasing a copy can do so by sending three strips of gold-pressed latinum to:

QUARK
c/o *Deep Space Nine*
Bajor Sector
Alpha Quadrant[*]

But to get back to the Rules. Don't let their simplicity fool you. Ferengi business scholars have been interpreting and debating them for thousands of years—ever since the first Grand Nagus, the gloriously devious Gint himself, wrote those immortal words, "Even in the

---

[*]Please allow six to eight weeks for delivery.

worst of times, someone turns a profit." Although that was, in fact, the first Rule of Acquisition ever committed to parchment, Gint, in a shrewd marketing ploy, labeled it the One Hundred and Sixty-Second Rule. Why? To increase the demand for the first one hundred and sixty-one. That Gint, always thinking.

Now, the way I see it, you have two choices. One is to carry this book with you at all times. That way, if you find yourself in the middle of a business negotiation, and you're not sure what your next move should be, you can whip out your copy of the Rules and thumb through it until you find an appropriate solution. Personally, I find this choice to be both lazy and inefficient. Your second choice is to do what I do. To do what all Ferengi do. Memorize the entire book. Okay, okay, I know that sounds a little daunting at first. But is it really?! I don't think so. All it takes is to memorize one Rule a day. That's not so bad when you think about it. In less than a year I was able to memorize all two hundred and eighty-five Rules. And you only have to memorize seventy. So the point is, if you want the Rules to work for you, you have to work on the Rules.

I know what you're thinking. Is it worth it? Will memorizing seventy Rules of Acquisition really make a difference in your life? Boy, you humans ask some pretty stupid questions. Of course it will make a difference. Aren't you tired of watching someone else make all the profit? Don't you wish you lived in a big house, had expensive possessions, went on fun-filled vacations? Of course you do. We all do. Well, here's your chance.

Look, don't be shy. Why don't you say what's really on your mind. After all, we're friends, aren't we? All right, I'll say it for you: "So far, Quark's made a lot of promises. How do I know I can trust him?" In other words, you want a guarantee that the Ferengi Rules of Acquisition will do everything I've said they will. Make you wealthier. Make you smarter. Make you more appealing. Don't worry. I'm not offended. It only makes me realize how desperately you need to learn these Rules. You want a guarantee? You need a guarantee? First turn to Rule Number Nineteen.

Go ahead.

I'll wait.

There, does that answer your question? Well, guarantee or no guarantee, the only thing you have to ask yourself is what do you have to lose? If the answer is nothing—and what other answer is there?—then you've got some reading to do. But before I send you off to get the most important education of your life, there's one last thing you should know. Ever since I decided to compile this book, my brother Rom has wondered why. Why am I doing it? Why am I willing to share the secrets of Ferengi success with a bunch of undeserving humans? Is it just to earn some extra profit? Is it to promote a better understanding between humans and Ferengi? Or is it to show an inferior race just how superior we Ferengi are?

The answer is none of the above.

The reason this book exists is because I have a dream. A dream of a brighter future that I firmly believe will change my life forever. A dream that will bring me greater profit than I've ever imagined. A dream that I am determined to turn into the greatest single business deal of my career. And that dream can be summed up in seven little words:

Quark's Ferengi Rules of Acquisition—
The Movie.

#1

Once you have
their money . . .
you never give it
back.

#3

Never pay more
for an acquisition
than you have to.

3

#6

Never allow
family to stand in the
way of opportunity.

#*7*

Keep your ears open.

#8

Small print leads
to large risk.

#9

Opportunity plus
instinct equals
profit.

#10

Greed is eternal.

#13

Anything worth doing is worth doing for money.

#16

A deal is a deal
. . . until a better
one comes along.

#18

A Ferengi without profit is no Ferengi at all.

#19

Satisfaction is not guaranteed.

#21

Never place
friendship above
profit.

#22

A wise man can hear profit in the wind.

#27

There's nothing more dangerous than an honest businessman.

#31

Never make fun of a Ferengi's mother . . . insult something he cares about instead.

#33

It never hurts to suck up to the boss.

#34

Peace is good for business.

#35

War is good for business.

#40

She can touch
your lobes but
never your latinum.

#41

Profit is its own reward.

#44

Never confuse
wisdom with luck.

#47

Don't trust
a man wearing
a better suit than
your own.

#48

The bigger the smile, the sharper the knife.

#52

Never ask when
you can take.

#57

Good customers
are as rare as
latinum—treasure
them.

#58

There is no substitute for success.

#59

Free advice is seldom cheap.

K eep your lies
consistent.

#62

The riskier the
road, the greater
the profit.

#65

Win or lose,
there's always
Huyperian beetle
snuff.

#75

Home is where the heart is . . . but the stars are made of latinum.

#76

Every once in a
while, declare
peace. It confuses
the hell out of your
enemies.

#79

Beware of the Vulcan greed for knowledge.

#82

The flimsier the product, the higher the price.

#85

Never let the
competition know
what you're
thinking.

#89

Ask not what your profits can do for you, but what you can do for your profits.

#94

Females and
finances don't mix.

#97

E nough . . . is
never enough.

#99

Trust is the
biggest liability
of all.

#102

Nature decays,
but latinum lasts
forever.

#104

Faith moves mountains . . . of inventory.

#106

There is no honor
in poverty.

#109

Dignity and an
empty sack is
worth the sack.

#111

Treat people in your debt like family . . . exploit them.

#112

N ever have sex
with the boss's
sister.

#113

Always have sex
with the boss.

#117

You can't free a
fish from water.

#121

Everything is for sale, even friendship.

#123

Even a blind man
can recognize the
glow of latinum.

#139

Wives serve,
brothers inherit.

#141

Only fools pay retail.

#144

There's nothing wrong with charity . . . as long as it winds up in *your* pocket.

#162

Even in the worst
of times someone
turns a profit.

#177

Know your enemies . . . but do business with them always.

#181

Not even dishonesty can tarnish the shine of profit.

#189

Let others keep their reputation. You keep their money.

#192

Never cheat a Klingon . . . unless you're sure you can get away with it.

#194

It's always good
business to know
about new customers
before they walk in
your door.

#202

The justification for profit is profit.

#214

Never begin a
negotiation on an
empty stomach.

#218

Always know
what you're
buying.

#223

Beware the man
who doesn't make
time for *oo-mox*.

#229

Latinum lasts
longer than lust.

#236

You can't buy
fate.

#242

More is good
. . . all is better.

#255

A wife is a luxury . . . a smart accountant a necessity.

#261

A wealthy man
can afford anything
except a conscience.

#266

When in doubt,
lie.

#284

D eep down
everyone's a
Ferengi.

#285

No good deed
ever goes
unpunished.

New rules are being revealed to you humans all the time. You can keep track of them here. Don't think this means you won't have to buy a revised and expanded edition of this book someday.

Rule #

_____

Rule #

_____

Rule #

_____

Rule #

_____

Rule #

_____

Rule #

_____

Rule #

_____

Rule #

_____

Rule #

_____

Printed in the United States
By Bookmasters